Spaced Out

by Lisa Thompson

illustrated by Bettina Guthridge

EDUCATION
Better ways to learn

Lexile® measure: 510L
For more information visit: www.Lexile.com

Spaced Out ISBN 978 1 86509 364 2

Blake Education Pty Ltd
ACN 074 266 023
Locked Bag 2022
Glebe 2037
Ph (02) 9518 4222
Fax (02) 9518 4333
Email: info@blake.com.au
Website: www.blake.com.au

Text copyright © 2000 Lisa Thompson
Illustrations copyright © 2000 Blake Education
Illustrated by Bettina Guthridge
Reprinted 2001, 2006, 2013, 2017
Lexile Copyright © 2013 MetaMetrics, Inc.

Series publisher: Katy Pike
Page layout: Artwork Express
Printed by 1010 Printing International Ltd

Jed

Comet

Jed's sister

CHAPTER 1

Jed in Space

Jed is space mad. His room is
filled with pictures of space and
spaceships.

There are glow-in-the-dark stars on the walls. Planets hang from the ceiling.

When Jed turns the light off at night, he feels like he is floating in space.

5

Jed spends a lot of his time looking at space through his telescope.

When the night sky is clear, Jed can see the surface of the moon. He can see different kinds of stars.

Jed's sister, Ali, thinks Jed is weird for looking up at space all the time.

"I don't know what you think is so interesting up there," Ali says.

"That's because your brain is a vacuum," says Jed. In space talk vacuum means empty.

Collecting Moon Samples

In the backyard there is a big
pile of rocks and sand. Jed thinks
it looks like the surface of the
moon.

With his dog, Comet, Jed spends hours collecting rock and sand samples. Like a real astronaut.

Jed has made his skateboard into a moon buggy. He uses it to collect his moon samples.

When Comet or Jed find something
they return to the spaceship. Here,
they inspect what they have found.

So far they have discovered three dog bones, a piece of limestone, two marbles and one old coin.

What Jed wants is a real piece of space rock.

CHAPTER 3

A Spaceship?

One night Jed sees something in the sky that he has never seen before. A big ball of light shoots across the sky. It's bright orange with a long tail.

It lands just behind the back
fence.

As scared as he is, Jed knows he has to go outside and take a look.

Jed hears noises on the other side of the fence.

"Aliens," he thinks.

Maybe it is a spaceship from another planet. What if the aliens have seen Jed looking through his telescope? They might take him away and throw him into a black hole.

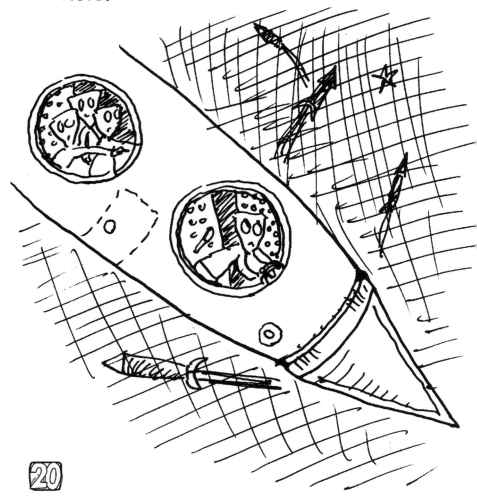

His dad has told him all about black holes. If you fall into one, you end up all long and thin like a piece of spaghetti.

Maybe they are friendly aliens and want to take him back to their planet. He would be famous. Then he could do whatever he wanted.

He would spend all his time travelling through space and going to new planets.

CHAPTER 4

Aliens

Jed finds a hole in the fence and
bravely climbs through.

"AHHHHHHHHHHHHHHHHH!" he screams.

The alien has a moon-shaped head, long hair and two big, brown eyeballs just like his own.

Jed closes his eyes and screams again.

"Stop screaming!" the alien says. It touches his shoulder. Jed screams even more loudly.

"Open your eyes," it orders.

Jed peeks out of his left eye.
Standing in front of him is his ...
sister.

"What's wrong with you?" she asks.
"You look all spaced out, like you
just saw an alien or something."

Jed's Mum and Dad and sister are all staring at him. Jed's dog, Comet, is too.

"Look Jed," says his dad, pointing to a hole in the ground, "a space rock has landed right here."

Space Rock

Three scientists come to look at the space rock. They do all kinds of tests.

Jed and Comet sit on the moon buggy and watch.

Finally, the scientists finish.

"Everything looks safe," they say.

One of the scientists hands the rock to Jed. "Here Jed, you can have it. It's a bit of a meteorite."

Jed can't believe it. "You mean I
can keep it?" he asks.

Jed runs inside to show the others.

"Look everyone. I get to keep the space rock. It's a meteorite."

Be Very Careful

Later, Jed finds his sister using his telescope.

"This space stuff is so cool. There's just so much to see. Can I have a look at the meteorite?" she asks.

Jed nods. He looks at her moon
face and big, brown eyes.

He has to be careful. Maybe his sister isn't a vacuum after all.

Maybe she is an alien.

GLOSSARY

alien
creature from space

astronaut
someone who
travels in space

inspect
to look at closely

meteorite
a rock from space

rock from space

samples
small parts or pieces

surface
the top layer

telescope
used to look at stars

vacuum
completely empty

weird
strange

Lisa Thompson

How high can you jump?

If I want, I can jump any size fence. No worries.

Why do ants have 6 legs?

Because when they got to the 'Things to Stick on Your Body' table, six ants legs was all that was left.

What is your favourite toy?

Lemon Twister — it makes you look really silly.

What is the hardest part of your day?

Looking for the keys time!

When did you write your first book?

I wrote my first book when I was about 8 about my mum losing her shoes when we went shopping.

Who was your hero as a child?

E.T. was my hero.

Bettina Guthridge

How high can you jump?

I don't like heights.

Why do ants have 6 legs?

So they can walk along tightropes.

What is your favourite toy?

My border collie called Tex.

What is the hardest part of your day?

When I have to be grown up.

When did you draw your first picture?

When I was bored.

Who was your hero as a child?

My grandmother.

my room

45